Kimberly V. Dwyer, Ph.D.
www.drkimdwyer.com

Printed in the United States of America
First Printing 2021
First Edition 2021

ISBN#: hardcover 978-1-7373253-2-1
paperback 978-1-7373253-3-8

For Cillian, always my baby owl
In honor of Sylvia and Ronald Vuillemenot

Baby Owl needed a new nest.
Even though he was small, and
the world was very, very large,
he wasn't really a baby any more.

It was time to be brave.
So, he set out on a Journey
to find a new home.

"Too-too-too!" sang Mom and Dad Owl,

and Brave Owl called back "too-too!"

Soaring the skies,
he looked for
the perfect tree...
Too **small**.
Too **bare**.
Too **lonely**.

Just right!

Brave Owl ✦
could see far and wide.
"Too-too-too!" he called,
announcing his new home.
He ate a delicious dinner and went to sleep.

"Chugga chug chug, Chugga chug chug."
The sounds drifted high up
to Brave Owl's nest.
"Hey Joe! Sharpen this saw so we
can get this big tree cut and loaded."

"Too- too- too too- too_too",
sang the saw on the whetting stone.

chugga chugga
chugga

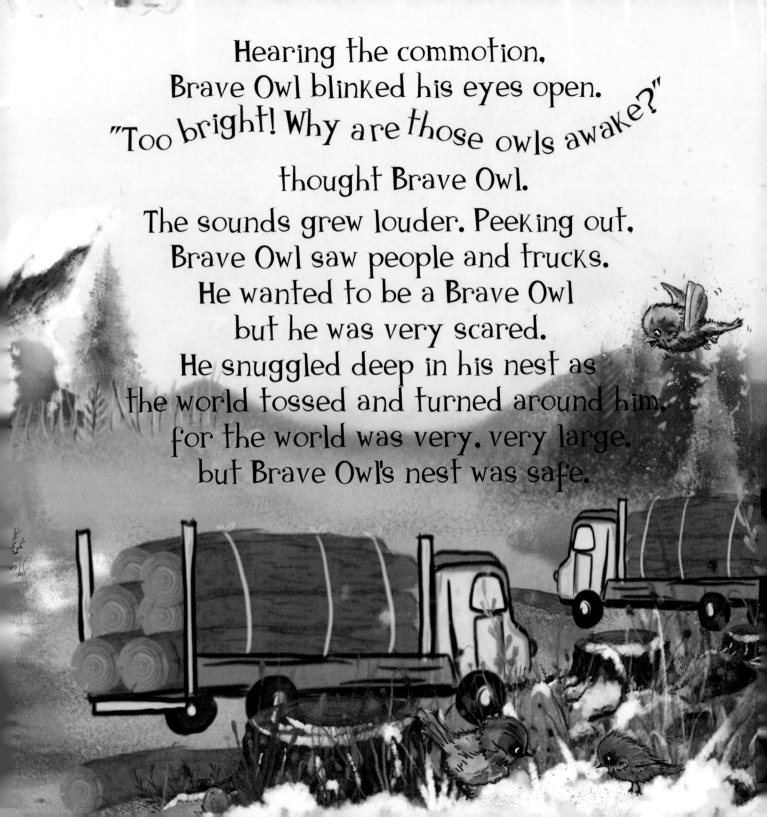

Hearing the commotion,
Brave Owl blinked his eyes open.
"Too bright! Why are those owls awake?"

thought Brave Owl.

The sounds grew louder. Peeking out,
Brave Owl saw people and trucks.
He wanted to be a Brave Owl
but he was very scared.
He snuggled deep in his nest as
the world tossed and turned around him,
for the world was very, very large,
but Brave Owl's nest was safe.

After a very long time,
the tossing and turning stopped
and the sky and ground were
back in the right spots.

The sideways nest gently rocked
Brave Owl back to sleep.

When Brave Owl awoke, his nest was right side up again!

He peeked out.

"This is not my forest.

These are not my stars.

Those are not my trees."

"Too-too-too!"
he called for his parents.
But they were far away now.
He wasn't Baby Owl
any more either.
He was just a lonely, Tiny Owl.
Tiny Owl in a big tree in the
very, very large world.

But then,
two gentle hands...

reached out...

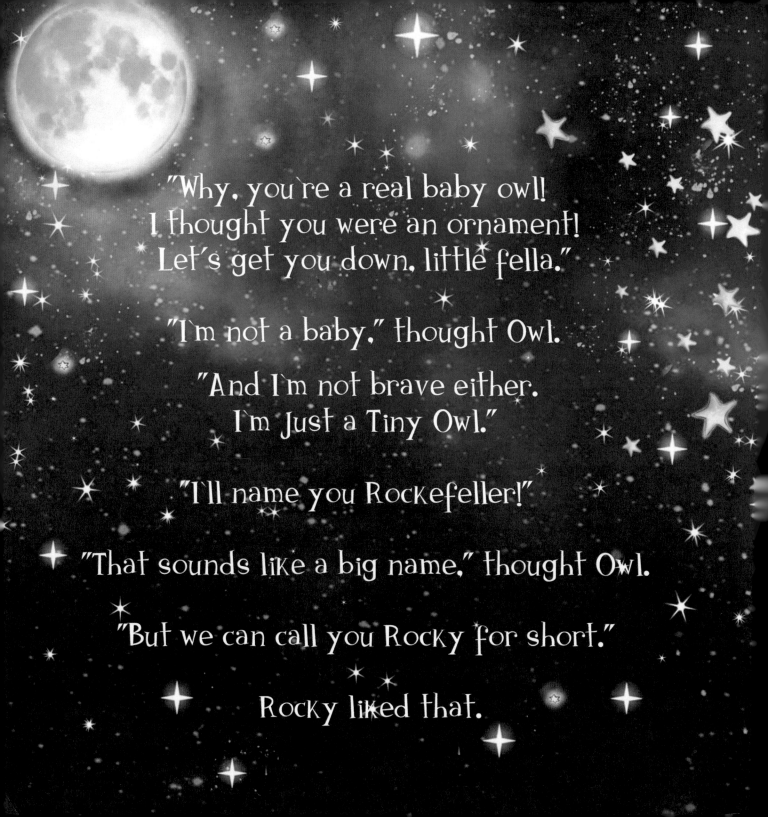

"Why, you're a real baby owl!
I thought you were an ornament!
Let's get you down, little fella."

"I'm not a baby," thought Owl.

"And I'm not brave either.
I'm just a Tiny Owl."

"I'll name you Rockefeller!"

"That sounds like a big name," thought Owl.

"But we can call you Rocky for short."

Rocky liked that.

"Come with me, Rocky.

You've got one more
Journey to take."

About Rocky

Rocky's Christmas Journey tells the imagined story of a very real owl who was discovered perched in the Rockefeller Plaza Christmas Tree in November, 2020. Rocky began his journey in Oneonta, New York, where he built his home inside a 75 foot tall Norway spruce. He must have been surprised and a little scared to take the unexpected 170 mile journey from his quiet pine forest to the lights and sounds of New York City! A worker securing the tree discovered Rocky, and arranged for him to be transported to the Ravensbeard Wildlife Center in Saugerties, New York, where orphaned and injured animals are nursed to health and returned to the wild. Rocky was determined to be an adult male Northern Saw-Whet Owl. Saw-Whet Owls were so-named because their "too-too-too" call is said to sound like a saw being sharpened on a whetting stone. Saw-Whet owls are one of the smallest species of owl in North America, earning them the nickname "the elf owl." They average a weight of only 2.8 ounces—roughly the weight of a deck of cards. Saw-Whets like Rocky live in conifer forests and eat small animals such as mice. The wildlife center gave Rocky lots of mice and fresh water to drink. After a few days, he had his strength back. A veterinarian examined him and found him to be in good health. Rocky was released into the wild to start a new journey.

Caregivers' Guide for Reading Rocky's Christmas Journey

I hope you are enjoying reading *Rocky's Christmas Journey* aloud. Reading together is a great activity for children and their caregivers, and promotes literacy skills. Rocky's tale also offers a rich opportunity for talking about imagination and feelings, and can serve as a springboard for future conversations. Here are some suggestions for questions to talk about with children after sharing this book. Use these questions as a launching point for rich conversations with your children to foster an understanding of feelings, reading comprehension, and real-world problem solving skills.

- How do you think Rocky felt when he left his nest? Why might he feel that way?
- What was Rocky's journey, and how did his name change on his journey?
- How do you think Rocky felt when he was looking for new trees, and when he found his perfect tree? How do you think he felt when he woke up and heard noises that he thought were other owls?
- How do you think Rocky felt when he realized he was not in his forest but in New York City? How do you think Rocky felt when the tree decorator picked him up, and how do you think the tree decorator felt when they found Rocky?
- How do you think Rocky felt when he was released from the wildlife center back to the wild? How do you think the people at the wildlife center felt?
- If an Owl was celebrating Christmas, what kind of gifts do you think they would like?
- If you were an Owl, what kind of tree would you want to make your home in?
- If Rocky could talk, what do you think he'd tell us about his journey?
- When Rocky woke up in New York City, he said "these are not my trees, these are not my stars." What was he looking at that was not trees or stars?
- What could you do if you find a wild animal that is lost or hurt?

About the Author: Dr. Kim Dwyer is an author and licensed clinical psychologist. She lives in suburban Denver, Colorado, with her husband, three sons, and three dogs. For more information, exclusive reader content, and to follow her work, visit her website at www.drkimdwyer.com.

Made in the USA
Columbia, SC
14 November 2021

48955137R00015